Let's Eat Healthy!

Can I Have a Snack?

Helena Markham

illustrated by
Aurora Aguilera

PowerKiDS press™

New York

Published in 2019 by The Rosen Publishing Group, Inc.
29 East 21st Street, New York, NY 10010

First Edition

Managing Editor: Nathalie Beullens-Maoui
Editor: Elizabeth Krajnik
Art Director: Michael Flynn
Book Design: Raúl Rodriguez
Illustrator: Aurora Aguilera

Cataloging-in-Publication Data

Names: Markham, Helena.
Title: Can I have a snack? / Helena Markham.
Description: New York : PowerKids Press, 2019. | Series: Let's eat healthy! | Includes index.
Identifiers: LCCN ISBN 9781508167969 (pbk.) | ISBN 9781508167945 (library bound) |
ISBN 9781508167976 (6 pack)
Subjects: LCSH: Snack foods–Juvenile fiction.
Classification: LCC PZ7.375 Ca 2019 | DDC [E]–dc23

Manufactured in the United States of America

CPSIA Compliance Information: Batch #CS18PK. For further information contact Rosen Publishing, New York, New York at 1-800-237-9932

Contents

I had a long day at school.

I'm happy to be home.

I'm hungry. Dinner won't be ready for 2 hours!

I ask Mom, "Can I have a snack?"

I want to eat a healthy snack.

I have lots of
healthy snacks
to choose from.

9

My favorite snack is called ants on a log. Mom spreads peanut butter on celery sticks.

Then I put raisins in the peanut butter.

Mom says she wants a healthy snack too. She cuts some carrots.

She puts some hummus
into a bowl.

13

14

Mom made pita chips
last week. She eats
those with the carrots
and hummus.

15

Dad comes in
from mowing the lawn.
He's hungry too!

16

Dad cuts slices of cheddar cheese.

He puts some grapes on his plate.

Our dog Percy wants a treat, too!

Mom gives him
a carrot.

We all sit around the table. Our snacks are so healthy! They'll keep us full until dinnertime.

23

Words to Know

celery

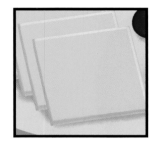
cheese

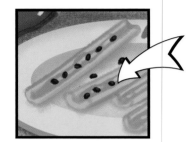
raisins

Index